Noddy
the Nurse

Collins

An Imprint of HarperCollinsPublishers

NODDY

CLOCKWORK MOUSE

BIG-EARS

MARTHA

TESSIE BEAR

GOBBO

MR PLOD

MASTER TUBBY BEAR

MONKEY

SLY

MR WOBBLY MAN

BUMPY DOG

It was a friendly afternoon in Toyland . . .

"Hello, Noddy!" Big-Ears said cheerfully when Noddy went to visit him. "I've just been thinking about Tin Can Day. It was a celebration we had in Toyland a long time ago, when I was very young!"

Big-Ears went on to describe how they had all collected tin cans and saucepans and kettles. Then, banging and clattering all the way, they would go on a procession to Stony Bridge and back to Market Square, where they would all eat hot chestnuts!

"It was believed that the banging and clattering would drive away all mischief-makers from Toyland!" Big-Ears explained.

Noddy was thinking what a lot of fun Tin Can Day must have been, when he suddenly had a wonderful idea.

"Let's have a Tin Can Day!" he said excitedly. "I should love to march around banging saucepans – and all the noise might drive away those mischievous goblins!"

Noddy and Big-Ears presented their idea to Mr Plod.
  As soon as they told him that a Tin Can Day
procession might drive away the goblins, Mr Plod was
very much in favour of it!

"Attention please, everybody!" Mr Plod announced loudly and importantly at Market Square. "Tomorrow will be Tin Can Day! All toys must come to Market Square with saucepans and kettles and... what else? Oh yes! Tin cans!"

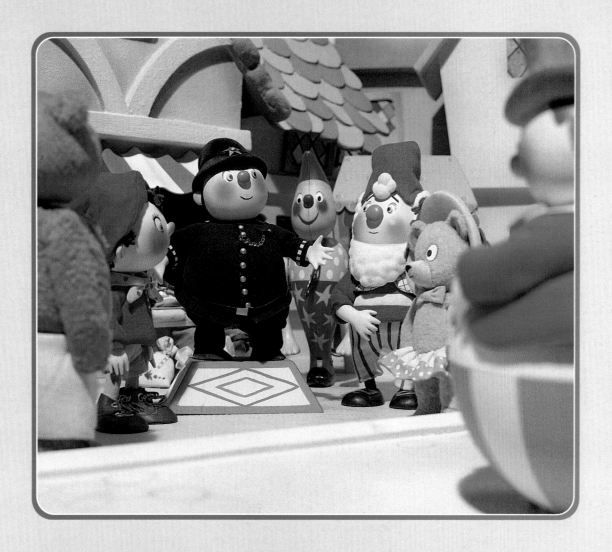

The toys were very excited about Tin Can Day, discussing it wherever they went.

"What a racket we'll make!" Mr Tubby Bear said to Jumbo. "Those naughty goblins will be driven right out of Toyland!"

Unfortunately, Sly and Gobbo overheard all this talk about Tin Can Day.

"They want to drive us away, Sly!" Gobbo cried. "Well, we'll soon see about that! Let's plan how we can ruin their silly procession!"

The next morning, all the toys gathered eagerly at Market Square with their pots and pans. Mr Plod got them ready for the procession.

"Into line, everyone!" he commanded. "It's time to move off!"

The toys had not marched very far, however, when they reached the first trap laid by the goblins. They had put dustbins right across the road!

Mr Plod quickly ordered everyone to halt...

But the toys were all making so much noise banging their saucepans and tin cans that no one heard Mr Plod. They all tumbled over as they marched into each other!

While all the toys were picking themselves up, the goblins were busy laying their next trap for the procession!

"This'll hold them up!" Gobbo smirked. "Now let's hurry to Stony Bridge to set the meanest trap of all!"

When Mr Plod saw all the branches across the road, he gave the command to halt.

But no one could hear him because of all the noisy banging. And again they all collided into each other!

The procession finally reached Stony Bridge, where the goblins had just finished laying their next trap.

"Now, according to custom," Mr Plod announced, "we will now be entertained by some acrobatic feats before returning to Market Square for our hot chestnuts. So entertain us, please, Clockwork Clown!"

Clockwork Clown stepped up on to the bridge to perform some acrobatic tricks. As he was about to flip up into the air, however, he slipped on some grease the goblins had poured on to the bridge.

Poor Clockwork Clown slithered right off the bridge and into the stream below!

Mr Plod dashed on to the bridge himself to try to grab
hold of Clockwork Clown.

But he just slithered all over the place as well!

They finally managed to pull Clockwork Clown out
of the stream, and he bravely insisted that the procession
should continue.

So they all marched back to Market Square, where Dinah Doll was ready to serve them hot chestnuts.

When Dinah Doll looked inside her special oven, however, she was horrified to see that someone had pinched all the chestnuts.

Of course – it was those bad goblins again!

There was even worse news. Clockwork Clown was to do some more tricks to entertain everyone, but he found that he could hardly move.

His arms and legs had gone very stiff!

"Perhaps you'll feel better, Clockwork Clown, after a warm and cosy night's sleep," Noddy told him kindly. "Would you like to stay at my house?"

Clockwork Clown was only just able to nod his head. "That would be so kind, Noddy," he said weakly.

"I'll put this warm blanket over you," Noddy said as Clockwork Clown made himself comfortable. "I'm sure you'll feel much better in the morning!"

But when morning came, poor Clockwork Clown felt stiffer than ever. Whenever he tried to move his arms or legs they made a loud creaking noise!

"You just need some breakfast," Noddy told him. "Would you like toast and eggs?" Clockwork Clown replied that his favourite breakfast was spaghetti.

"Then I'll go straight to the market to buy some!" Noddy said.

Clockwork Clown thought Noddy was so kind. He was just like a nurse!

As he drove to the market, Noddy noticed that his car was making a strange creaking noise.

"You sound just like Clockwork Clown!" he exclaimed. "I'd better take you to Mr Sparks' garage!"

"Nothing to worry about, Noddy!" Mr Sparks told him as he peered underneath the car. "Your back wheels are just a bit stiff. A spot of oil will soon put it all right!"

Then Noddy suddenly remembered that Clockwork Clown was very stiff today as well. Perhaps he just needed a drop of oil too!

"Will you come to my house and oil Clockwork Clown, Mr Sparks?" Noddy asked hopefully.

"Of course!" Mr Sparks replied.

While Clockwork Clown was eating his spaghetti, Mr Sparks put a drop of oil on each of his legs. Then he put a drop on his arms and neck as well.

"There you are, Clockwork Clown!" he exclaimed cheerily. "You're fully oiled!"

Clockwork Clown carefully stood up and tried a little hop. In no time at all he was jumping all around the room!

"I feel better than ever!" he cried with delight.

Clockwork Clown could not wait to do his acrobatics again, so Noddy took him to Market Square.

As everyone gathered round and cheered at Clockwork Clown's cartwheels, Noddy had a great idea.

"Since yesterday's Tin Can Day was ruined," he cried, "let's have another one!"

The only toys who did not enjoy the new Tin Can Day were Sly and Gobbo.

They could not bear all the banging and clattering!

"Look at your coat, Sly!" Noddy cried as they all surrounded the goblins. "You've spilt grease on it!"

"So it was you two naughty goblins who poured the grease all over Stony Bridge!" Mr Plod exclaimed.

He tried to arrest them, but Sly and Gobbo ran off – far, far away from Toy Town. They did not like the horrible noise and they did not like going to prison!

All the toys cheered as they watched the mischievous goblins disappear.

"It looks as if Tin Can Day has worked again after all!" Big-Ears chuckled.

This edition first published in Great Britain by HarperCollins Publishers Ltd in 2000

1 3 5 7 9 10 8 6 4 2

Copyright © 1999 Enid Blyton Ltd. Enid Blyton's signature mark and the words
"NODDY" and "TOYLAND" are Registered Trade Marks of Enid Blyton Ltd.
For further information on Enid Blyton please contact www.blyton.com

ISBN: 0 00 136184 8

Reproduction by Graphic Studio S.r.l. Verona
Printed in Italy by Garzanti Verga S.r.l.

MORE NODDY BOOKS FOR YOU TO ENJOY

Noddy and the Artists

Noddy and the Bouncing Ball

Noddy is Caught in a Storm

Noddy and the Driving Lesson

Noddy is Far Too Busy

Noddy and the Goblins

Noddy and the Magic Watch

Noddy and the Noisy Drum

Noddy and the Singing Bush

Noddy Tells a Story

Noddy Tidies Toyland

Noddy and the treasure Map